BUILD REX'S MINIFIGURE—HE'S A SPACE ADVENTURER WHO WILL
HELP EMMET GET OUT OF COSMIC TROUBLE.

HEY, I THINK I'M LOST!
CAN YOU BUILD SOMEONE
THAT WILL HELP ME OUT?

WHO WILL EMMET ASK TO HELP HIM? USE THE CLUES BELOW TO FIND OUT!

IT DEFINITELY WON'T BE A DUPLO CREATURE!

THIS PERSON IS NOT A PIRATE . . .

. . . DOESN'T HAVE ANY HORNS . . .

. . . WEARS A MASK . . .

. . . AND ISN'T WEARING BLUE!

LUCY

UNIKITTY

DUPLO CREATURE

BENNY

BATMAN

METALBEARD

WHICH ROUTE SHOULD THE FRIENDS TAKE TO REACH BATMAN'S BASE? ADD THE POINTS ON EACH PATH AND YOU'LL FIND OUT THE ANSWER. THE ROAD WITH THE LEAST POINTS WINS.

HOW MANY?

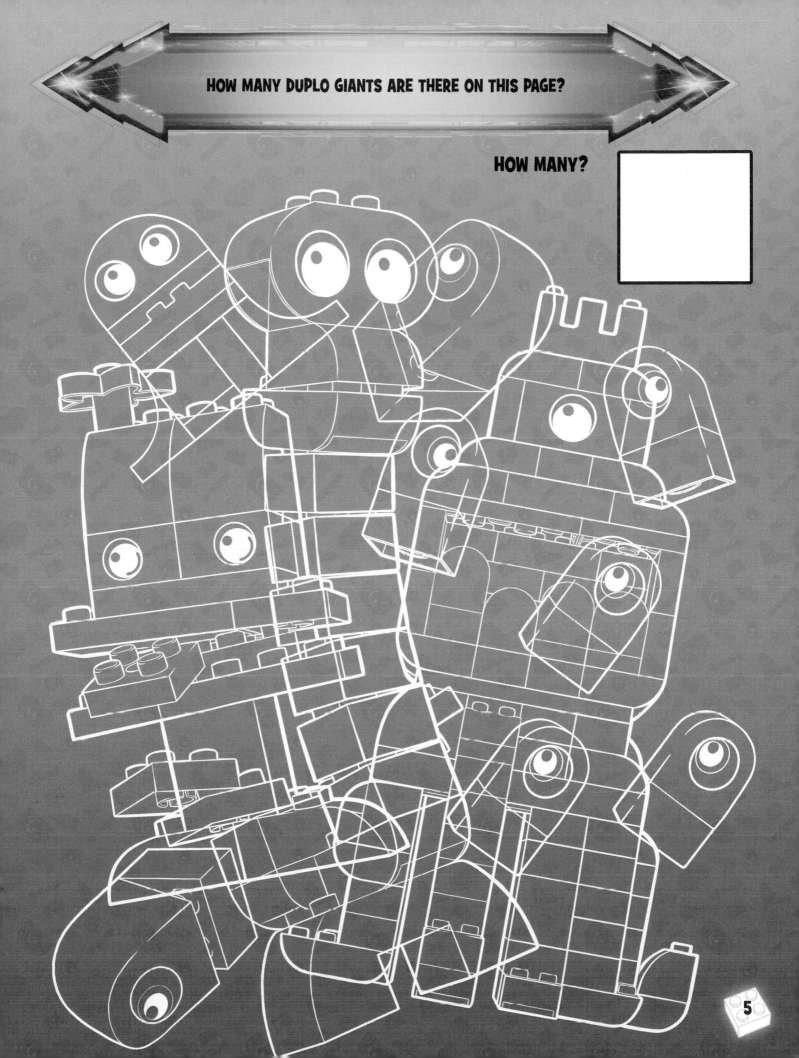

FIND A CREATURE IDENTICAL TO THE ONE IN THE BLUE BOX.

WHO IS EMMET THINKING ABOUT AS HE RUNS AWAY FROM THE DUPLO CREATURES? THE CHARACTER APPEARS TWICE IN HIS THOUGHT BUBBLE.

BATMAN IS READY TO ATTACK! HE JUST NEEDS TO FIND SOME THINGS IN THIS MESS: SEVEN BATARANGS, TWO GRAPPLE GUNS, AND THE KEY TO THE BATMOBILE.

LOOK AT THE PICTURE BELOW AND FIND THE FRAGMENTS FROM THE CIRCLES. MARK THEM WITH A CORRESPONDING LETTER. NOTE: TWO LETTERS ARE USED TWICE!

I GET LOTS OF ANGRY THOUGHTS WHEN I LOOK AT THE GENERAL ON THE NEXT PAGE!

WHICH OF THE HELMETS IS IDENTICAL TO THE ONE THAT SWEET MAYHEM IS WEARING?

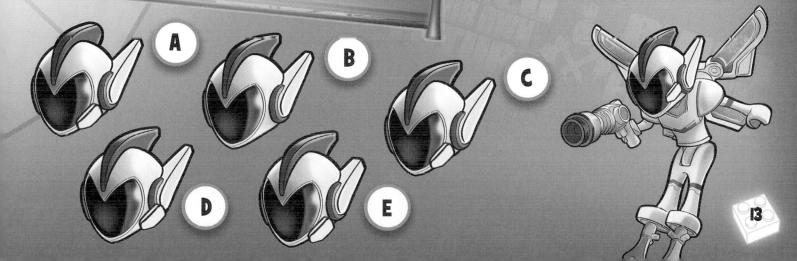

A

B

C

D

E

DESIGN A MACHINE OR VEHICLE YOU THINK WOULD HELP DEFEAT
THE MYSTERIOUS SPACESHIP!

TO BUILD IT YOU WILL NEED PARTS
OF YOUR OWN DESIGN AS WELL
AS: A BANANA, TWO CANNONS, AND
FOUR PIZZAS.

SWEET MAYHEM IS CONTINUING THE ATTACK. DRAW TWO STRAIGHT LINES TO DIVIDE THE WHITE RECTANGLE INTO THREE PARTS, WITH TWO STARS AND TWO HEARTS IN EACH PART.

WE LOVE YOU.

I LOVE YOU.

COMPLETE THE SEQUENCE OF THE GENERAL'S POSES AT THE BOTTOM OF THE PAGE BY WRITING THE CORRECT LETTERS IN THE BLANK SPACES. NOTE THAT ONE LETTER IS NOT USED.

A   B   C   D

16

SWEET MAYHEM HAS TAKEN THE HEROES! UNTANGLE THE LINES TO SEE WHO AVOIDED BEING TAKEN.

EMMET IS SETTING OFF ON A JOURNEY TO SAVE HIS FRIENDS. FOLLOW THE ARROWS INDICATING THE DIRECTION AND THE NUMBER OF SQUARES YOU NEED TO MOVE. YOU'LL SOON REACH SWEET MAYHEM'S VEHICLE.

START

18

MATCH THE MISSING PUZZLE PIECES TO THE PICTURE OF EMMET FLYING IN HIS SPACESHIP.

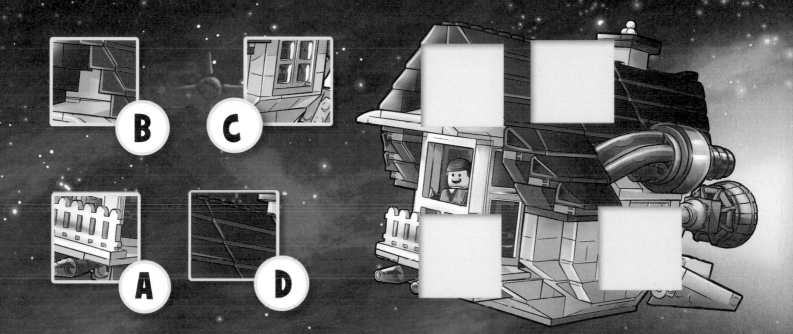

LOOK AT THESE SHAPES AND CHOOSE THE ONE THAT MATCHES EMMET'S VEHICLE.

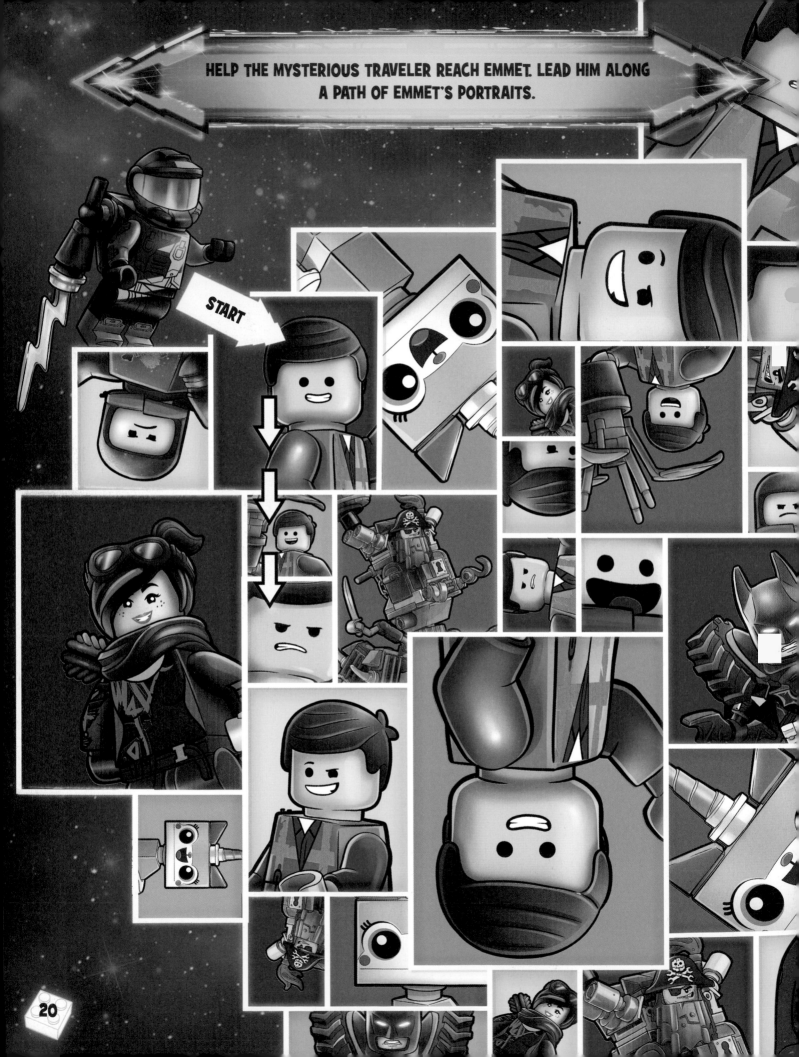

HELP THE MYSTERIOUS TRAVELER REACH EMMET. LEAD HIM ALONG A PATH OF EMMET'S PORTRAITS.

START

HURRY UP! WE'VE GOT A MISSION TO COMPLETE!

FINISH

21

VEST FRIENDS OR NO, YOU'RE MY HERO!!!

YOU'RE MY HERO, MAN!

HEY! THIS IS REX. HE SAVED ME!

REX IS AN ADVENTURER, AN ARCHAEOLOGIST, A COWBOY . . .

AND ON TOP OF THAT, HE'S A RAPTOR TRAINER! HOW COOL IS THAT!?

HIS SPACESHIP IS ENORMOUS! AND IT'S CALLED REXCELSIOR! THIS GUY IS THE BOMB!

HAVE YOU EVER TRIED DRAWING A RAPTOR TRAINER? HERE'S YOUR CHANCE!
FOLLOW THE INSTRUCTIONS BELOW.

SKETCH THE PROPORTIONS USING
GEOMETRICAL SHAPES.

1.

DRAW THE CHARACTER'S SHAPE WITH
A THICKER LINE.

2.

ADD THE EYES AND THE MOUTH.

3.

DON'T FORGET THE STUBBLE!

4.

HEY! PRACTICE HERE!

TO CONVINCE THE HEROES TO STAY WITH HER, QUEEN WATEVRA
WA'NABI PROMISED EACH OF THEM THE THING THEY DREAMED OF.
CONNECT THE DOTS TO SEE WHAT THINGS SHE PROMISED BENNY
AND METALBEARD.

NOW DRAW THE THINGS SHE MIGHT HAVE PROMISED LUCY AND UNIKITTY.

SHE'LL NEVER GUESS WHAT I'M DREAMING OF!

27

PLEASE REX! HELP ME REACH THE SYSTAR DIMENSION AND RESCUE MY FRIENDS.

I'M NOT GOING BACK THERE! IT MADE ME FEEL SO LONELY!

COME ON, IF YOU TEACH ME HOW TO BE TOUGH, WE CAN BE A TEAM.

OKAY, THAT SOUNDS GOOD! FASTEN YOUR VEST. THROUGH THE STAIRGATE TO THE SYSTAR DIMENSION WE GO!

I SUSPECT YOUR FRIENDS WERE TAKEN BY AN ALIEN QUEEN AND THEY'RE ON ONE OF THESE PLANETS. JUST TELL ME WHICH ONE.

ME?

SURE! YOU ARE THE SPECIAL AND YOU DECIDE.

WHAT IF I'M WRONG?

JUST POINT TO ONE OF THE PLANETS AND BE CONFIDENT. THAT'S WHAT THE SPECIAL DOES.

OK! LET'S SAY IT'S . . . THIS ONE!

HA! I KNOW THIS PLANET! IT'S FULL OF HOSTILE ALIENS, WHO DREAM OF TORMENTING . . .

. . . AND BRAINWASHING US. IT'S GONNA BE SO MUCH FUN!

I CAN'T WAIT!

UMM . . . I JUST REALIZED THE SPECIAL DIDN'T CHOOSE THE RIGHT ONE! CAN I HAVE ANOTHER GO?

ANSWERS

2-3

4-5

6-7

8

9

12-13

15

16–17

18–19

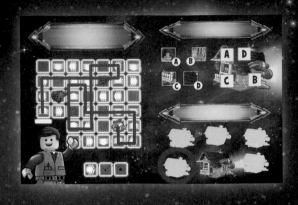

20–21

26–27

30